Pat Cat and Max

Just Right Reader

Look at Pat Cat in a cab.

Pat Cat has a bag.

Pat Cat has a hat in the bag.

Pat Cat has a map in the bag.

Pat Cat looks at the map.

Max?

Look at Max!

Can Max see Pat Cat?

"Max!"

"Pat Cat!"

Phonics Fun

- Use magnetic letters or create your own on individual squares of paper: a, b, c, g, m, n, p.
- Use the letters to make words from the list.
- Make and read each word.

bag   cab   can   map

 ## Comprehension

Would you tell a friend to read this book? Why?

 ## High Frequency Words

has   see
look   the

 ## Decodable Words

bag	hat
cab	map
can	Max
cat	Pat